WHERE'S BUDDY?

WHERE'S BUDDY?

RON ROY

Drawings by Troy Howell

AN
APPLE®
PAPERBACK

SCHOLASTIC INC.
New York Toronto London Auckland Sydney

Thanks to Dr. John B. Wells and
Dr. Richard Harrison-Atlas for reading
the manuscript of this book and for their
helpful suggestions; and to Dianne Hess for
her insight, tact, and diligence in preparing
the book for publication.

ISBN 0-590-32985-5

12 11 10 9 8 7 6 5 4   6 7 8 9/8 0 1/9

*This book is lovingly dedicated to
Ian the wanderer and Brendan the fetcher.*
R.R.

1

Mike Sanders peeked out from beneath his blanket. He slowly opened his eyes and focused on the sea gull sitting in his window. He watched the large gray bird attack the ear of corn and chunk of garlic bread, the remains of Mike's supper from the night before.

Mike called the bird Seabreeze. He'd been feeding her every summer for three years, since his family had started renting the house in Ogunquit, Maine.

Like a kitten attacking a leaf, Seabreeze rose into the air and pounced on the corncob with both feet. Mike laughed, caught himself, and held his breath. Too late. Seabreeze pinned Mike with her beady gold eyes, gave an annoyed squawk, and catapulted herself into the morning sunlight.

Mike knew the bird would be back later that day to finish what she'd left. He stretched and yawned loudly, but made no move to get out of his bed. He was on summer vacation with nothing to do but swim, fish, ride his bike . . .

He bolted up off his pillow. It's Saturday, today is football! But his watch said eight-thirty so he dropped back down and hooked his hands behind his head. The game was scheduled for ten-thirty. Plenty of time.

One of the high school coaches organized touch football games every Saturday in the summer. Only the games were more like gang pillow fights than scrimmages.

Coach Bing invited everyone to play: young and old, short and tall, male and female. And he always got a crowd. Mike would rather have played real football, but Coach Bing's games were a lot of fun. Mike hadn't missed a Saturday game in three summers.

He reached up behind his head and banged on the wall. If Buddy was awake in his room he'd knock in return. Then Mike remembered what time it was. His seven-year-old brother would be downstairs having breakfast by now.

Buddy was a diabetic. He had to eat breakfast every morning at the same time, eight o'clock. Regular meals, morning and afternoon snacks, and insulin four times a day kept him alive. For reasons Mike didn't understand, Buddy's pancreas couldn't produce its own insulin. So he'd been getting insulin injected into him, through needles, for five years.

Mike shuddered. He was glad he wasn't a diabetic. Buddy's doctor had told Mike that sometimes more than one child in the same family got the disease, but so far none of the symptoms had shown up. Mike knew them by heart: loss of weight, weakness, extreme hunger, having to urinate often.

Mike sat up. He reached a long leg over the

edge of the bed, clamped his toes onto a pair of cut-off jeans, and drew them up and under the blanket. His leg snaked out again for a T-shirt, but his foot found only cool bare floor. Rats.

As he drew on his shorts, he hopped across the floor to a sunny spot under the window. Even though the morning was chilly, Mike knew it would be hotter than the inside of a sneaker by noon. He gazed out at the ocean where the sun was turning the water to silver. A few small boats were out already, adding color to the gold and silver morning.

Mike loved this old house his parents rented every summer, and he loved the view from his room. It was like one of the paintings that hung in the art gallery in town.

He grabbed a T-shirt from his drawer, zipped up his shorts, and headed for the stairs leading down to the kitchen. In his house, if you didn't show up on time for meals, you'd end up with the leftovers like Seabreeze.

Mike slid into the old church pew that served as kitchen seat for him and Buddy. He gave his brother a nuggie in the back of the head as he sat down. A nuggie is a fast knuckle rub in the hair, sure to cause friction. He clamped his right arm to his side to ward off Buddy's elbow, which was the response he expected to the nuggie. Mike was surprised when it didn't come.

Buddy sat stone-faced, staring at a bowl of soggy Cheerios. Mike's father was bent over a yellow pad, scribbling with a black Magic Marker. Next to him Mike's mother sat reading out loud, with a mug of tea in one hand and a catalogue from an antiques dealer in the other.

" 'Wedding dress, circa 1882, white organdy with lace, and hat to match: $125.00; hat pin collection, fifty assorted, circa 1875: $150.00; seven men's top hats, beaver, circa 1900: $75.00 each.' "

"Too much," Mike's father mumbled, raking long fingers through his beard. "I'll offer half."

"Start lower," his wife suggested. "Let the dealer bring you up to half."

13

Mike listened to his parents' familiar chatter. They had been in the antiques business ever since he could remember. Their summers were only part vacation. They spent a lot of time searching out good buys to take back to Connecticut where selling prices were much higher. It looked as if today was a buying day for *Sanders' Sundries, Inc.*

Mike glanced at Buddy, still pulling a long face over his cereal bowl. "What's wrong with you?" he asked, filling his own bowl with granola.

Buddy sniffed, slid lower in his seat, and said nothing. But his message came out loud and clear. He wasn't getting his way about something.

Mike's mother lowered the catalogue. "Buddy is annoyed with us because we want to take him along today. We're going to Sleeping Giant to an antiques show." She reached out and tousled Buddy's curly blond hair. "There'll be other kids, darling, and lots of food. You'll have a wonderful time."

"It'll be boring," Buddy whined. "I want to stay home with Mike." He wiped at a tear that hadn't shown up yet. The rest of his family exchanged looks. When Buddy got into one of his moods, the world could gather at his feet in worship and he'd still insist that nobody loved him.

Mike followed a spoonful of cereal with a gulp of juice. "You can't stay with me because I'm not going to be here. I'm playing football at the high school. Game starts at ten-thirty."

"So, I could go too." Buddy sat up a little straighter and abandoned his poor-little-Buddy act for the time being.

Mike looked at his brother and sighed. Buddy was a neat little guy, but spoiled. Ever since it was discovered that he had diabetes, everyone had fallen all over themselves to make sure he was happy.

When the doctor warned the family to treat Buddy like any other kid, nobody listened. Even aunts, uncles, and cousins back home treated Buddy as if he were a little prince. Mike had been guilty, too. Now, if Buddy didn't get his way, out came the lower lip and down came the tears.

"If you come with me you have to promise to do what I say and not pull any scenes," Mike said.

"What time is your game over, Mike?" his father asked. "Remember, Buddy has to get lunch and his shot by one-thirty."

"We'll be back by then, no sweat."

"Will you listen to your brother, Buddy?" his mother said. "We should be back by three o'clock."

Buddy nodded happily. He looked like one of those toy dogs you see in the rear windows of cars. The dog's head is suspended on a little hook and as the car moves, the head goes crazy bobbing up and down.

So it was decided. Mike's father printed the times on a sheet of yellow paper: morning snack—10:00; game with Mike—10:30; lunch—1:00; insulin—1:30. Leaning back in his seat, he made a place for his note among the other recipes, reminders and newspaper clippings already attached to the refrigerator door with magnets.

Mike was glad the doctor had insisted that Buddy learn to give his own injections. He and his parents had been taught also, but the doctor said Buddy needed to be responsible for his own medication. Buddy had been injecting himself with insulin for two years.

At nine o'clock, Mike helped his parents load the station wagon with items they'd brought from their store in Connecticut to sell or trade in Maine. Back in the house, he found Buddy sitting in front of an opened coloring book. But he wasn't coloring. He was slowly peeling the paper from a bright orange crayon. His freckled, stubborn little face wore one of his far-away-from-Earth looks.

Mike stood looking down at his brother. *Now* what's Buddy up to? he wondered.

2

"*C*an Pete come to the high school, too?" Buddy asked.

So that's it, Mike thought. It was Petey Anderson Buddy wanted to stay home for. The Andersons were townies, which meant that they lived in Ogunquit year round. Petey was a year older than Buddy, but they got along like two puppies from the same litter.

"You little turkey," Mike said. "If you wanted to stay home and play with Petey, why didn't you just say so at breakfast?"

"I didn't think Mom would let me stay home if you didn't watch me. Can he come?"

"Okay, if I have to look out for one squirt, I might as well look out for two." Mike headed for the kitchen to fix himself more breakfast. Cereal just didn't fill him up. "Go ahead, give Pete a call."

"I did."

Mike stopped in the doorway. "When?"

"While everyone was outside loading the car."

"So?" Mike asked. "Is he coming or not?"

Buddy stripped the last bit of wrapping from the orange crayon. He began slowly coloring in one eye of a tyrannosaurus rex. "His sister says he can't play football because he got hurt last year."

Mike remembered the incident. Pete had collided with somebody's head. The nosebleed stopped after a few minutes, but Petey went home with a bloody T-shirt. Obviously, the Andersons remembered too.

"Well, if Pete can't come, he can't," Mike said. "But we're leaving here right after your snack."

Buddy left his dinosaur with one orange eye and followed Mike into the kitchen. "I bet if you ask Loni she'll let Pete come," Buddy wheedled, staring at Mike with his puppy eyes. "I think she likes you," he added.

Mike didn't go for the bait. He kept his back to Buddy while he prepared snake eyes for his second breakfast.

He'd learned to make them on a scouts camping trip. You needed the biggest frying pan in the house, two slices of bread, and two eggs. You melted a little butter in the pan, cut a round hole in the middle of each piece of bread, then fried the bread in the butter. While the bread was frying you dropped an egg (without the shell!) into each hole. After one minute you flipped the bread and eggs over. Wait another minute and presto, snake eyes.

"So will you?" Buddy persisted.

"Will I what?" Mike selected an egg from the carton. Crack. Plop.

"Will you call Loni and ask her to let Pete come to the high school with us?"

"Yep, if you do something for me." Crack. Plop.

"What do I have to do?" A sudden wariness had crept into Buddy's voice.

Mike grabbed the spatula from its hook over the stove. "Wash the frying pan and my plate when I'm done eating."

"Neato!" Buddy ran out of the room and came back with the Ogunquit telephone directory. He slapped it down next to Mike's plate, left again, and returned with his coloring book and a fistful of crayons. While Mike ate, Buddy neatly filled in each scale on the dinosaur with a different color.

"What's that supposed to be?" Mike asked, glancing across at the rainbow-colored creature.

"Tyrannosaurus rex."

"Looks more like tyrannosaurus mess."

"Did you ever see one?" Buddy asked.

"No," Mike sighed. "They all died when I was just a baby."

"Then how do you know what they look like?"

22

"Forget it," Mike mumbled. How could he win an argument with a seven year old?

As Mike mopped up the yolk with another slice of bread, Buddy stood at his elbow, waiting. Mike pretended to be absorbed in wiping the last trace of food from his plate.

"Mmmm, that was so good, I'll have two more," he said, rubbing his stomach. He turned to Buddy. "Waiter, bring me two more snake eyes, please."

Buddy was too fast. He whipped the plate out from under Mike's hands and dropped it into the sink. He turned again and shoved the phone book in front of Mike where the plate had been.

Mike sighed and flipped the book open to the A section. "Get started on the dishes," he said, glancing at his watch. "It's ten of ten. And be thinking about what you want for your snack."

Mike found the number, memorized it, and left the kitchen to make the call. He flopped on the sofa with the phone on his chest and dialed.

"Hi," he said into the mouthpiece. "This is

23

Mike Sanders. Is Loni home? Oh, it is. Well, my little brother asked me to call you. He really wants Petey to come to the football game to-day. I said I'd call and ask."

Mike listened as Loni explained for the second time that Pete had to stay home. She was watching him until her parents got home from playing golf. And one bloody nose was enough, thanks.

"Uh . . . can you hang on for a second?" Mike cupped his hand over the phone and yelled toward the kitchen. "Buddy, come here a minute."

Buddy strolled out of the kitchen with soapy water dripping from his elbows to his wrists to his fingers to the floor.

"Pete's sister says he has to stay home," Mike whispered. "She's supposed to sit for him till her folks get back. So what do you want me to say?"

Buddy hesitated only a second. "Can I go over there?"

Mike watched the two little puddles of

water grow bigger. Why not let Buddy go over to Pete's for a couple of hours? he asked himself. I could drop him off at ten-fifteen and pick him up again after the game.

Mike waved his brother back to the kitchen as he put the phone to his mouth. "Clean up that mess or Mom's going to kill you," he said. "What? Oh, not you. That was my brother. He was washing the dishes and got water all over and then . . ."

Mike's voice petered out and he could feel his face turning scarlet. He gathered his wits and spoke into the phone again. "Listen, Buddy really wants to play with Pete today. Is it okay if they play at your house for a couple of hours?"

Buddy yelled from the kitchen just as Mike hung up. "Is it okay? Can I go?"

"Yeah. She didn't sound too happy about it, but she said you could come." Mike bolted for the stairs. "Now hurry up. We're leaving in twelve minutes."

"I didn't finish the dishes."

Mike peered into the kitchen. "Geez, Buddy! What are you trying to do, wash the whole house?"

Buddy stood on a chair with his arms buried in a mound of white, quivery soapsuds two feet tall. It looked as if he were being swallowed by the sink monster.

"Forget the dishes and find something for your snack," Mike muttered, turning toward the stairs. "And don't forget your you-know-what."

Buddy's you-know-what was his urine test. After meals he was supposed to urinate on a little plastic stick his mom got from the doctor. If the color of the stick stayed the same after it was wet, everything was all right. But if the stick turned darker or changed color, it meant something was wrong.

Mike decided he'd better use the bathroom himself. Once the game started it would be too late. Before leaving the upstairs bathroom, he poked at his corn-colored hair and squinted his eyes into the mirror to make his freckles look like tan.

26

His freckles refused to cooperate. Mike sighed. Freckles are freckles, he decided, and tan is tan. He flicked off the light, then remembered something and hit the switch again.

He slid the medicine cabinet open. Buddy's insulin supplies lined the bottom shelf where he could reach everything. There was a jar of alcohol-dipped cotton balls for wiping his skin; ten or fifteen disposable syringes standing in a juice glass; six or eight small vials of insulin; and a jar of sticks for testing urine. The cabinet in the downstairs bathroom contained the same set of equipment.

Mike's mother checked both bathrooms every morning to make sure nothing was missing. Mike and his dad checked the shelves, too. The only one who wasn't interested was Buddy. He seemed content to let his family worry about his "tool kits."

Mike slipped into his sneakers and hurried down the stairs to find Buddy shoving half a banana into his mouth. A jar of peanut butter and a loaf of bread stood on the table next to the banana skin.

"You ready?" Mike asked.

"Don't you want to know if I went to the bathroom?"

Mike rolled his eyes. "Sure I want to know. Did you remember to test?" He found it embarrassing to discuss Buddy's urine tests.

"The stick turned purple with green spots," Buddy said, trying to keep a straight face.

"Terrific," Mike said, dumping the banana peel into the trash. "Maybe you're turning into a salamander. Now can we please go?"

"I told you, I just went."

"What a comedian! You should be on the stage." Mike put his hand on the back of Buddy's neck and hustled him toward the door. "Come on now, get on your bike."

Buddy rode and Mike jogged the half mile to Pete's house. Like their rental house, the Andersons' place had been built near the cliff above the ocean. Mike filled his lungs with the salty sea air as he ran along the edge of the cliff. The sight of the waves crashing below made his heart pump in time with his legs.

If only he could get rid of the small pang of

guilt he had about leaving his brother with Loni Anderson, everything would be perfect. His worry was silly, he knew.

What could happen to him in the next two hours?

3

A dense grove of tall pines separated Loni's street from the cliff and the ocean. As Mike loped along the path through the trees, he noticed that they had been bent away from the sea by the wind.

He slowed to get his breath and to let Buddy catch up. Looking back into the dark tunnel under the trees, he saw Buddy's bike emerge, wobbling in the soft pine needles. Seeing him hunched over the handlebars, all business and pedaling like mad, Mike had to smile.

When they reached her house, Loni was sitting on the front porch. Mike waved, but Loni didn't seem to notice.

"Hi," Mike puffed. He jogged in place so she'd get the idea he was in a hurry. "I'll pick Buddy up around twelve-thirty, okay?"

Loni was about Mike's age, but that's where the resemblance ended. He was skinny with long arms and legs. She was more rounded; her shirt and jeans fit her snugly. Mike had blond hair, light eyes, and skin. And freckles. Loni's hair and eyes were as black as a crow's feathers. She stared at him while he bobbed up and down in front of her. She still hadn't said a word.

"And I want you to know," Mike went on as if they'd been having a conversation, "that I really appreciate this."

"And I want *you* to know that at exactly twelve-thirty I'm sending Buddy and Pete to your house for two hours while I go to the beach." Loni flashed a cool smile.

Now Mike really felt guilty. Was she mad? He felt her eyes on him, but instead of returning the look he bent down and tied a sneaker that didn't need tying.

"Be a good kid," he said to Buddy. "Do everything Loni says, okay? And I'll see you at the house at twelve-thirty." He looked, finally, at Loni. "Where's Petey?"

"Here I am." Petey Anderson came strolling around the corner of the house. His hands and the pockets of his shorts were filled with miniature toy soldiers and Indians.

"We can have a battle," Petey said when he saw Buddy. "But I'd rather go play football," he added, giving his sister an icy glare.

"Well, you're not going, so just get the idea out of your scheming little brain." Loni stood up and from the top step looked down at Mike. "Be seeing you, Sanders."

Mike stood with his mouth open as she disappeared behind the screen door. Slam.

"Be seeing you, Sanders!" Buddy chirped. He and Petey, hysterical with giggles, tore around to the back of the house.

So that was that. Mike shook his head. Why was Loni acting so unfriendly, he wondered. Looking after Buddy for a while wasn't *that* big a deal, was it? On the phone she'd sounded, while not exactly friendly, at least reasonable.

He didn't have time to brood about Loni right now. He glanced at his watch and started running back the same way he'd just come. It was almost ten-thirty, but knowing Coach Bing, the game would start late.

Mike was right. When he arrived at the field, puffing hard and feeling the heat, only about fifteen other players were there. Coach Bing told everyone to relax until a few more people showed up.

Mike gave the coach his watch for safekeeping and flopped on his back in the grass. Big puffy clouds floated across the sky, changing their shapes as they moved. Mike picked out an alligator, two pirates in a boat, a redheaded monster in a striped rugby shirt.

That one was his best summer friend, Chick Dawson. He'd come to play and was standing over Mike and making faces.

"What're you doing, anyway?" Chick asked, dropping to his knees.

"Resting. It was a rough game."

"What? You mean it's over?"

Chick believed anything and everything. Mike could never resist teasing him. He was still chuckling when the coach blew his whistle for the people to choose sides. There were always an equal number of little kids, medium-sized kids, and adults on each team.

The teams lined up and squared off. No hard blocking was allowed, but Mike and Chick played their own game within a game. They faced each other across the white line in the grass.

"Get ready to eat dirt," Chick growled.

"If you hurt me I'll tell the coach," Mike answered in a high squeaky voice.

The whistle screeched. Hank Gerassi's mother centered. In slow motion, a giant purple nerf ball flew high over the heads of the players.

The game had begun.

The ball bounced off little Christy Wilson's head and was caught by old Mr. Cheney who ran the hardware store. He started running for all he was worth.

"No, no, you're going the wrong way!" his team screamed.

"Not wrong," Mr. Cheney puffed in answer. "Closer!" Everyone cracked up and the coach gave Mr. Cheney's team a touchdown.

That's the way the whole game was played. Most of the time people were laughing so hard they couldn't run or catch. Sometimes players changed from one team to another to add to the confusion.

The coach kept score, but sometimes he forgot who had done what, so he made up the numbers. When that happened, everyone yelled like crazy and the coach acted as if he were hard of hearing.

At last the coach blew one long blast on his whistle. The game was over. Chick's team won, 72 to 28. Mike's team chased the coach off the field, but stopped when he dragged a big thermos bottle of lemonade out of his car. Everyone cheered, gathered for cups, and found places to rest.

Coach Bing walked over to where Mike and Chick were sitting in the grass. "Here's your watch, Mike," he said. "You know, you're as tall as some of my freshmen. What do they feed you at home?"

"It's all the beer he drinks," Chick offered. "And of course he loves worms, spiders, old sweat socks . . ."

Mike leaped on top of Chick and tried to feed him a fistful of grass.

"Hey, your watch, be careful." the coach rescued the watch and put it in Mike's hand.

"Thanks for saving my life, Coach," Chick said, spitting out grass.

Mike sat on Chick's stomach and stared at the watch as the second hand jerked its way around. It was twelve-forty. "Oh no! I was supposed to be home ten minutes ago!"

Mike rolled off Chick, leaped to his feet, and sprinted across the field. He cut across Hubbard Street, leaped the fence in front of Alice's Fish Market, and headed toward the ocean. Using every shortcut he knew, it would still take him ten minutes to get home.

He slowed from a sprint to a jog when he saw his house. Both the front and back of his T-shirt were stuck to his skin with sweat. His hair was plastered to his forehead. Even the waist of his cutoffs was damp.

Mike swept his eyes along the broad front porch of the house, but he didn't see Buddy or Pete. He ran around back and checked the pile of sand where his brother sometimes played. The boys weren't there, either.

Beginning to worry, Mike raced to the edge of the cliff where his backyard dropped away. If Buddy's down there on the beach I'll kill him, Mike thought. But all he saw on the sand were two sea gulls ripping at a dead fish.

"BUDDYYEEEE!" Mike yelled, swiveling his head. His voice was swallowed up by the louder sounds of the ocean. He ran to the house and leaped up the back porch steps. Maybe Buddy and Petey were inside shoveling down sandwiches and cookies.

"Are you guys in here? *Hey, are you guys here?*" Mike's voice bounced off the walls, but no one answered his call. In the kitchen, the table and counters looked the way he remembered them from the morning.

He threw himself onto a bench and dug his hands into his sweaty hair. His heart was beating faster than it usually did from a run. Damn. Where could those kids be? He glanced at the stove clock. Ten of one. Still forty minutes till Buddy was supposed to get his insulin. *But where was he?*

Calm down, Sanders, Mike told himself. They have to be here someplace. Buddy has never forgotten his insulin since he was four years old. Could he be hiding somewhere? Punishing me for being late?

Starting in the hall off the kitchen, then continuing upstairs, Mike searched every room, closet, dark corner and cubbyhole in the house. Buddy was nowhere to be found.

Back in the kitchen, Mike sank onto a bench and covered his eyes to think. His hands were shaking. If they had left Pete's house at twelve-thirty, they'd have gotten here about ten minutes later. Okay, so they got here and they didn't find me. So what would they do? They . . . they'd go back to Pete's! Mike raced for the telephone in the living room.

He had to dial three times because his finger kept slipping out of the holes. When he finally completed dialing Loni's number, the phone was busy. He slammed the receiver down; picked it up; dialed again. Still busy. "Get off the phone!" he yelled.

Then he had a better idea. He'd ride over to the Andersons' on his ten speed. That would take less than five minutes. He strapped on his watch and raced to the side porch where he kept his bike.

Dropping to his knees, he worked the combination lock: right twenty . . . left thirty . . . right ten. Mike yanked on the lock, but it remained shut. He ignored the sweat trickling into his eyes, but wiped his shaking hands on his shorts before trying the numbers again. This time when Mike tugged it, the lock popped open.

He decided to take Main Street instead of following the cliff as he and Buddy had earlier. He'd make better time on pavement than in sand. But he stopped before he left the front yard. Throwing down his bike, he raced back through the house and into the bathroom.

He flung open the medicine cabinet, grabbed a vial of insulin and a box of syringes, and stuffed them into his pockets. As he hurried through the house again, the clock in the living room sounded.

It chimed just once, for one o'clock.

4

The sound of the striking clock made Mike's stomach turn over. In another half hour it would be time for Buddy's shot. What can I do, he asked himself. Get to Loni's. Buddy had to be there.

Mike rode hard, pumping in the fastest gear. Down Main Street, along South Main, past the yacht club and the boat factory. When he turned down Loni's street, he aimed for her house, barely missing a dog asleep on the sidewalk.

He rang the bell, waited two seconds, and then began pounding on the door. At last Loni threw it open. She was wearing a bathing suit. "What's going on?"

"Is Buddy here?" Mike knew the answer by the startled look on Loni's face.

"What do you mean? I sent them to your house."

"They aren't there. I was late. I have to find Buddy—he has to get his insulin."

"They aren't at your house? What are you talking about?" Loni's face turned white. *"Where's my brother?"*

"I told you, I don't know. I got home and they weren't there. I was late . . . I . . . couldn't help it," Mike explained. His hands were wet. "Listen, will you help me look? Buddy has to have his shot."

Loni stared into Mike's face until what he'd just said registered. "They aren't at your house and they aren't here. Where could they be?"

"I don't know," Mike said for the second time. "Buddy had his bike—did he leave it here?"

"No, they both took their bikes when they

left. They wanted to go early, about twenty after. Maybe they're just riding around the
neighborhood."

"Uh-uh," Mike said. "Buddy knows he gets
his insulin every day after lunch. I told him to
be home at twelve-thirty. You heard me, remember?" Mike's face was burning. He'd also
told Buddy that *he'd* be home then to meet
him.

Loni slid her eyes away from Mike's face
and stared over his left shoulder. "Indians,"
she said softly. "They were talking about playing Indians. Pete took a bunch of his toys when
he left." She looked at Mike again. "Where are
your mom and dad?"

"They went antique hunting. They won't be
home till around three." His parents. What
would they say when they found out he'd
shoved Buddy off onto Loni for the morning?
The one time they needed to rely on him and
he'd screwed up. Mike's stomach went sour.

"Listen, can I use your phone?" Mike dug
his wallet out of his back pocket. He prayed the

paper was there. It was, folded and tucked behind the picture of himself showing off a fifteen-inch trout. Mike's mother made him and Buddy carry the number, just in case.

Loni showed Mike to the phone in the kitchen. "Who are you calling?"

"Buddy's doctor, the one we use while we're in Maine." He dialed carefully and heard the ringing of the doctor's telephone. It sounded far off. Someone picked up on the fifth ring.

"Doctor Williams's answering service."

Answering service! Of course, it was Saturday. Doc Williams was probably playing golf, or at the beach. Mike felt sick as he spoke into the receiver.

"I need to talk to Doctor Williams. It's about my brother, he's a diabetic. He's supposed to get a shot in twenty minutes and he's disappeared."

"Doctor Williams won't be in until Monday," the voice said. "Doctor Benjamin is covering for him. Hold on and I'll try to locate him for you."

Mike switched the phone into his other hand and wiped the sweat from his palm. The temperature in Loni's kitchen seemed to have gotten fifty degrees hotter.

"Doctor Benjamin here," a voice said into Mike's ear.

Mike told the doctor his story, then answered the questions that came over the phone like bullets:

"Where are your parents?"

"Out. They'll be home at three."

"When did your brother have his last injection?"

"Seven-thirty this morning."

"His last food?"

"Ten o'clock; a banana and a peanut butter sandwich."

"How old is your brother?"

"Six . . . no, seven. He's seven."

The doctor stopped firing questions. Mike heard his breath coming through the earpiece, slow and regular.

"You have until about two-thirty before

your brother will be in trouble," the doctor said. Mike closed his eyes. Trouble could mean anything—even death. Doc Williams had explained it: Buddy had to have his insulin or else.

The doctor was speaking again. ". . . talk to his pals; look anywhere he's apt to be playing. Call back if you need me."

Mike hung up, shaken. He wanted to walk out of Loni's kitchen and go . . . he didn't know where.

Instead he opened the telephone book again. This time he was looking for the number of the Ogunquit police department.

5

Loni listened as Mike described Buddy and Pete to the police. "What did they say?" she asked when he hung up.

"They're going to radio the descriptions to the cruisers," Mike said. He wrapped the phone cord around his hand until his fingers started to turn purple. "He said they might even put a few extra guys on to help search."

"What are we supposed to do, just wait?" Loni looked scared. Mike wondered if it was for Buddy or Pete.

"No. The guy said the same thing the doctor told me: Check the schools and playgrounds, anywhere kids hang out."

Mike's eyes followed Loni's as they flicked to the wall clock. It was one-eighteen. "Look," she said, tracing the tablecloth pattern with one tapered fingernail, "if they went to your house when they left here, they'd have gotten there about twelve-thirty, right? What time did you get there?"

Her question sounded like an accusation. Mike knew he deserved it. "I was about fifteen minutes late, why?"

"Because maybe when you didn't show up they decided to go for a walk or something. Why don't we check your house again before we go running all over town?"

Mike twisted on the kitchen stool. Loni was right. Buddy might be sitting at home right now, waiting. "Okay, let's go." He stood up. "Do you have a bike?"

Loni nodded. "I'll put on some jeans and meet you around front. Don't lock the front door," she added, "in case they come back here."

The ride back to Mike's house took six minutes. According to his watch, it was just one-twenty-nine when they got there. They dumped their bikes and sprinted across the yard. Mike ran into the house while Loni circled the house on the outside.

Mike searched the bottom floor, then took the stairs three at a time. But it was no use hurrying. The house was just as empty as it had been at one o'clock.

When Mike came downstairs he found Loni on the back porch. "Look." She held out her hand. In her palm lay a toy Indian; he was crouched, tomahawk over his head, as if ready to scalp someone. "It was on the step," Loni said. "This means they came here. It's one of Pete's Indians."

Mike stared at the Indian, wishing it could speak. "Come on, we have to try the schools. They might be at one of the playgrounds."

"There are four," Loni said. "Pete goes to Ogunquit Elementary, but that leaves the middle school, the junior high, and the high school."

"We'll split up," Mike said. "You take Pete's school and the middle school. I know where the others are. Where should we meet?"

"Why not here?" Loni asked. "Wouldn't Buddy have to come here for his shot if . . . when you find him?"

Mike patted his front pockets. "I've got the stuff, but let's meet here anyway." They compared watches. Loni's was a little faster. While she set it to match Mike's, he closed his eyes and clenched his jaws to fight off the panic he was beginning to feel. "Let's go," he said.

"What about the pool?" Loni said. "Shouldn't we check there?"

"I will, on the way to the junior high." Mike snatched up the telephone book. "I just had another idea." He dialed the number for the town library. When he was connected to the children's room, he told the librarian that Buddy Sanders and Pete Anderson were missing. He asked her to please ask all the kids who came in to keep an eye out for them. If anyone saw them, they were to go to Buddy's house right away. And stay there.

Mike and Loni rode off in opposite directions on their bikes. Mike was glad Loni was helping him look for Buddy. He wondered if she'd be so willing if her own brother weren't with him. He guessed she would be; she was an all-right kid.

Mike didn't feel quite so panicky since Dr. Benjamin had told him Buddy could go another hour beyond one-thirty without insulin. With the police looking, and the library notified, maybe everything would be all right. Maybe.

When Mike braked in front of the town pool, his hopes fell apart. He sat on his bike, stunned by the sight in front of him. Every kid for ten miles around seemed to be in the water. The ones who weren't were sitting on the edge waiting, or using the playground equipment. Finding Buddy in this crowd would be impossible.

Mike heard the shriek of a lifeguard's whistle. "NO RUNNING NEAR THE POOL. NO RUNNING OR YOU'RE OUT!" Mike watched the guard set the megaphone on a bench and stick the whistle between his teeth.

For five seconds there was complete silence in the pool.

With his bike leaning against a tree, Mike ran to the pool. When he touched the guard's arm, it was hot. "Can you help me?" Mike asked.

"What do you need?"

When Mike told him, the lifeguard stared at him the same way Loni had earlier. "You serious?"

Mike nodded.

Suddenly the whistle screamed again. Two hundred wet bodies froze. The guard raised the megaphone to his mouth and pressed the talk button. "BUDDY SANDERS, IF YOU'RE IN THE POOL, YELL OUT. BUDDY SANDERS, ARE YOU IN THE POOL?"

Heads turned; shoulders shrugged. Nobody yelled out. The lifeguard lowered the megaphone and looked at Mike. "Sorry, kid. I guess he's not here."

Mike's legs felt rubbery. "Could you try the playground?"

The guard turned away from the pool and raised the megaphone again. He asked Buddy Sanders to come to the pool immediately.

A few heads swiveled, but Mike didn't see anyone running or biking toward him and the guard. He swung his gaze back to the pool. Hundreds of kids were staring at him. With the sun on their wet hair and skin, they all looked alike. "Thanks anyway," he mumbled to the guard and ran back to his bike. He had wasted time, but at least he could forget about the pool.

As he threw his leg over his bike, Mike realized how tired he was. He glanced at the pool; the water was the color of a robin's egg. It would feel great to do a cannonball off the deep end.

Instead Mike locked his feet onto the pedals of his ten speed and headed for the junior high school.

Ten minutes later Mike swung into his yard and pedaled toward the back. His shirt hung limp from a back pocket. A pain behind his eyes made his head throb. He saw Loni sitting on the back steps and flung himself down next to her.

He stared at the ocean to avoid looking at her. A lone sailboat sat on the still water. Its sail hung lifeless, waiting for a breeze.

Mike's stomach cried for food, but he felt too sick to care. He knew Loni was watching him; he also knew she hadn't found the boys, either.

Inside the house the phone rang. They both jumped, then froze, staring at each other. Could this be it? Mike raced into the house and caught the phone on the third ring. "Hello?" His heart sounded louder than his voice.

"Mike? It's Mom. I tried calling around one o'clock but no one answered."

Mike bit his bottom lip to keep himself from crying. His mother chattered on.

"I just called to see how you two monkeys are doing. Everything all right? Did Buddy—"

Mike took a deep breath and interrupted. "Mom, I've got something to tell you. . . ."

6

*L*oni looked up as Mike stepped onto the porch. His face was white. "Who was it?" she asked.

"My mom," Mike whispered. "I told her. They're coming home." He lowered himself to the steps on legs no longer able to support his weight. His mind had been a mess before the phone call. Now he couldn't think at all. He looked at Loni. "Did you have any luck?"

Loni stared at the ground and shook her head. "There were only a few kids at the playgrounds." She couldn't look at Mike. "No one has seen Buddy or Pete."

She scuffed a trench in the sand with the heel of her sneaker. The sand poured slowly back into the hole, and an ant scrambled for its life.

Mike stared at the insect. That's how he felt: trapped. At least the ant knew what to do.

"I can't stand this!" Loni cried. "They have to be somewhere!"

She turned to face Mike. "Help me think. They played with Pete's Indians and soldiers under the tree in our backyard. I sat near them reading. I went inside for a drink; when I came out they were whispering. They stopped, but when they thought I wasn't listening they started again."

Loni closed her eyes to remember. "They were pretending to be real Indians. They were going to eat Indian food and talk Indian talk and . . . they mentioned a cave where they would sleep and . . ."

"There is a cave," Mike interrupted. "About half a mile from here. Buddy's not allowed to go there alone."

"Where is it?" Loni asked. "I never heard of any cave around here."

"It's at the bottom of Bald Head Cliff. My friend Chick showed it to me and Buddy last summer."

Mike and Loni looked at each other, each thinking the same thought. "They were whispering about it," Loni said. "I thought it was all make-believe."

Mike was already moving toward his bike. "Let's go. We can ride there in five minutes."

He pedaled across his yard toward the cliff. Loni caught up and they rode single file. Sixty feet below them, waves crashed over the rocky beach.

Mike slowed a little and yelled over his shoulder. "You'll see an old tree. That's Bald Head Cliff."

He had jogged this path a hundred times. He knew every rock, every patch of sun-browned grass and cliff-hugging bush. To his right the cliff dropped into the ocean, then there was nothing until you got to Spain. On his left were open fields of wild grass, blueberry bushes, and granite boulders the size of Volkswagens. A few people lived there, but their homes were beyond the fields.

On other days Mike liked to pretend he was an Olympic runner in training as he loped along this path. Today he thought only of his destination.

The wind from the ocean roared over the top of the ridge in sudden gusts. Mike hunched low over his handlebars and Loni copied him. This position changed her angle of vision so she

was looking straight ahead instead of down. She never saw the stone on the path.

Mike heard the sound of metal slamming into rock and Loni's scream at the same time. He braked and whipped his head around. Loni's bike lay in the dirt. The rear wheel spun, humming like an angry hornet. The front half of the bike was resting on Loni's right arm and shoulder.

Mike jumped off his bike and let it drop to the ground. By the time he reached Loni, she was on her feet.

She was holding her right hand with her left. Both hands were shaking. Particles of dirt were imbedded in the flesh of her right palm. Blood oozed from the skin around the dirt.

Mike felt helpless. His own hands hung at his sides like anchors. "Does it hurt?"

"No, it feels terrific," Loni blurted. She was trying not to cry, but Mike saw her eyes water over and tears start to slide down her face. Her jeans were torn at one knee and the front of her T-shirt was covered with dirt. "Is my bike okay?"

Glad for something to do, Mike raised her ten speed. He held the handlebars and sighted with one eye along the bike's length. Nothing was bent. He walked the bike a few yards along the path, then back again.

"I think it's all right," he said. "But what about your hand?"

"It's just the palm," Loni said, carefully brushing at some of the imbedded dirt. "How much farther is the cave?"

"Can you ride?" Mike asked.

"Don't worry. I can make it," Loni answered.

Mike had his doubts. "Listen, I have an idea. You could go back to my house and wait. Maybe the kids . . ."

Giving no hint that she'd heard, Loni yanked her bike from Mike's hands, swung into the seat, and pedaled away. Toward Bald Head Cliff.

Mike stood with his mouth open. She's amazing, he thought as he retrieved his own bike from the dirt. He had to pump hard to catch up; Loni was yards ahead of him.

7

The pine tree was the only living thing on Bald Head Cliff. Like most of the trees along the ridge, it was stunted and misshapen. Years of wind had twisted the branches, and salt, carried by the wind, had left them bare except for a few withered pine needles. The tree pointed away from the sea, as if in warning.

Two small bikes leaned against the trunk of the tree.

The relief of seeing the bikes propped there made Mike's eyes water. Buddy and Pete were here. In minutes the nightmare would be over.

Mike yelled to Loni, who, he guessed, hadn't

noticed the bikes yet. "They're here!"

Loni's face burst into a smile. Mike felt his own grin spread as Loni dropped her bike and ran toward the tree. Then Mike remembered the cave, and his grin vanished.

Most of Mike's summer friends knew about the cave. At first they'd all thought Indians once lived in it, but they'd found no signs of early inhabitants: no arrowheads, no pottery, no wall pictures. Just a tunnel you had to crawl on your belly to get through and a medium-sized cave at the end.

Mike hated the cave. Ever since he could remember, any cramped dark place made him feel as if he were being smothered. Only Chick's persistent urging had persuaded Mike to crawl into the tunnel the first time. That had also been the last time.

The darkness was the worst part. Not knowing how much space was around him made him think he was running out of oxygen. Mike would never forget the sensation of suffocating.

Loni's voice broke into his thoughts. "Mike,

come over here!" She was standing at the edge of the cliff, pointing at something on the beach.

Leaving his bike alongside hers, Mike ran to where she stood. When he looked down he understood why she had yelled. The beach was completely covered with water. And the beach was the only way to get into the cave.

Mike dropped to his hands and knees and moved to the very edge of the cliff. Just below where he crouched the rock bulged out; from the beach it looked like a giant forehead, bald except for the lone tree.

Mike couldn't tell how deep the water was on the beach. He tried to recall whether the tide had been high or low, incoming or outgoing when he'd looked out his window that morning. But he couldn't remember—too much had happened since then.

He looked for a way down and saw what he wanted. Twenty yards away a small path left the ridge and zigzagged down to the water. With Loni right behind him, he began picking his way down.

The cliff was steep, but they found hand-

holds and toeholds in the crumbly, eroding rock. Mike wondered if Buddy and Pete had climbed down this same path.

He couldn't take his eyes off the dark water below. Now that he was closer, it didn't look too deep. But it was coming in fast. Everyone, townies and summer people, knew about the Ogunquit tides.

Mike looked back at Loni. Her face was white, and she too had eyes on the water. He noticed that she was using both hands to keep herself from sliding.

Four feet from the bottom of the cliff, Mike jumped. The shock of the cold water made him clench his teeth. He knew the numbing pain would go away in a few minutes, but now he felt as if he were walking on needles. His sneakers didn't help a bit.

He was right about the depth of the water; it was just above his ankles. In a half hour it would be up to his waist.

Loni crouched at the spot from which Mike had jumped. She looked at Mike, then leaped into the water. Her eyes opened round when the impact hit her. "It's freezing!" she cried.

Mike backed away from the cliff until he was knee-deep in the swirling, sucking water. He flicked his eyes back and forth along the base of the cliff.

"There it is!" With arms flailing to help keep his balance, he splashed his way toward a black hole in the rock face about fifty feet away.

Loni followed. She kept her left hand on the cliff and held her right one against her stomach. Her eyes never left the water churning around her ankles.

Mike dropped to his knees at the tunnel entrance. He stuck one hand in the water and leaned the other against the rocks. He lowered his head and peered into the tunnel opening.

"Buddy! Are you in there? Buddy, Pete, answer me!" Mike heard only the muffled sound of his own voice. And the roar of the Atlantic behind him.

Loni leaned close to his ear. "What are you going to do?"

Mike felt her arm against his knee under the

water. Her flesh felt cold, like the dead frogs in science class. "I'm going in."

Loni put her hand on his shoulder and shouted. "I can't hear you. What did you say?"

"I said I'm going in," Mike yelled back.

Loni lowered herself until the water slapped at her stomach and wet the ends of her hair. She peered into the dark hole. "I'm coming with you."

Mike stared at her. There was no way he could tell her the relief he felt at not having to face the tunnel alone.

"We'll have to crawl on our stomachs," he shouted. "The tunnel slopes up, so it should be dry most of the way. What about your hand?"

Loni held her palm up so Mike could see. "It got cleaned off in the water. It doesn't hurt anymore."

Mike swiveled on his knees and faced the ocean. Somewhere he'd heard that every seventh wave was bigger than the other six. To him they all looked the same.

Turning, he threw himself into the icy water and crawled into the mouth of the tunnel. He felt like one of the prehistoric lizards in Buddy's coloring book. The only part of him still dry was the top of his head. Everything else was soaked.

Suddenly he stopped. The tunnel was too narrow for his elbows and knees. He realized, lying in the dark and shivering, that he'd grown a lot since last summer. He and Chick had crawled in easily then.

Something touched Mike's leg. He jerked forward, then relaxed. It was Loni. He felt her breath on his ankles. Her wet hair tickled his skin.

"Can't you move in any farther?" she yelled. "My legs are still in the water!"

"I can't crawl," Mike yelled over his shoulder. "My stupid arms and legs are too long."

Loni didn't say anything for a few seconds. Then Mike heard a gasp and violent choking. Icy fingers grabbed his leg.

"Mike!"

"What's the matter?"

"A wave hit me," Loni said through chattering teeth. "I'm freezing. Can't you pull yourself along with your hands? I can't stay here."

Mike reached ahead and dug his fingers into the sand. Using his toes to push off with, he was able to move forward an inch at a time. He could hear Loni scraping along behind him.

Having her with him kept the panic away. He was scared, but he knew he wasn't going to smother. His breaths came easy. Somehow, knowing Buddy was waiting made a difference, too. He didn't want to scream and kick his way out as he had the other time.

Mike turned his head until his hair brushed the tunnel wall. "You okay?"

"I think I cut my knee on something," Loni answered. "But at least I'm out of the water. How about you?"

"I'm all right," Mike said. "Let's keep moving."

With Loni blocking out most of the sounds from the ocean, Mike heard only the noises their fingers and toes made digging into the sand. He established a system: stretch forward, dig in, pull, shove off . . . stretch forward again. His arms and shoulders began to ache. His

72

muscles weren't used to this kind of exertion.

He stopped and laid his cheek in the cool sand. Loni's breathing told him she was getting a workout, too.

Something crawled over Mike's hand. He yelled, jerking it back.

"What's the matter?" Loni asked.

The back of Mike's neck felt as if it had been doused with ice water. He was sure his heart had stopped altogether. And all for nothing. He felt foolish.

"I think we've invaded a crab's home," he said. "One just walked over me."

"Crabs? Yuck! If one touches me I'll—"

"Shhh . . . quiet! I heard something." Mike's skin prickled all over. He held his breath.

He heard the sound again. "Didn't you hear it?" he asked Loni.

"I can hardly hear *you* back here," she said. "What is it?"

He waited till he heard the noise one more time. Then he was sure. He had heard the sound of someone crying.

"It's them. It's Buddy and Pete!"

8

Mike cupped his hands and yelled into the darkness. "BUDDY, PETE . . . ARE YOU IN THERE?" He waited, but heard nothing except his own breathing.

"Maybe it was something else," Loni offered. Her voice sounded ghostly in the cold black space.

"Like what?" Mike asked.

"I don't know . . . a sea gull?"

At any other time Mike would have laughed at the thought of a sea gull living in a tunnel. But now he didn't even smile. "Let's go," he said. It *had* sounded like crying.

The short rest helped; Mike was able to hitch himself along more easily. He didn't forget Loni's remark about the sea gull. What if some animal *were* living in this cave? Why not? It was a perfect spot: away from the water and safe from enemies.

What lived in caves, he asked himself as he inched cautiously along. Bears? Yes, but they'd never fit in this tunnel. Skunks? Snakes? He drew his arms under his chest at the thought. He'd never been afraid of snakes, but putting his hand on one in the dark was a different matter.

Loni shoved his foot. "Why did you stop?"

Mike ignored her. He reached into the darkness, dug his fingers into the sand, and hiked himself forward. Look out snakes, here I come!

He realized that his head was no longer grazing the roof of the tunnel. One hand reached out but there was nothing to touch. He pulled his knees in under his rear and raised his arms over his head. He struck rock.

"What are you doing?" Loni whispered.

"The tunnel is wider here," Mike said. "I think we're close to the cave."

He heard a crunching noise, then felt Loni's hand on his back. She snuggled near him. "I wish I could see."

"I should have brought matches," Mike said. He reached down to check his pockets anyway. The only lumps he felt were the insulin and syringes.

"Come on," he muttered. Suddenly an explosion of light blinded him. He threw his hands up to protect himself. Loni screamed and grabbed his legs.

As fast as it had appeared, the light vanished. Mike heard a thumping, dragging noise. Something crashed into him and past him, making choking noises as it moved. Then Mike heard a cry from Loni.

"Petey! Petey, it's you!"

Loni's brother had crawled out of the darkness. She and he were both crying and trying to talk at the same time.

Mike groped until he found Petey's arm. "Pete, where's Buddy? Is he all right?"

Pete's sniffing and sobbing quieted. Mike

smelled something familiar; it was peanut butter.

"Buddy fell asleep," Pete said. "I couldn't
wake him up. I knew the tide was coming in
and we had to leave, but he stayed asleep."

Mike's head began to spin. He squeezed
Pete's arm tighter. *"Where is he?"*

"Back there," Pete answered. "I heard you
guys talking and I . . ."

"Give me the flashlight," Mike snapped. He
felt Pete's hand searching for his, then the
metal touched his skin. Mike flipped the light
on, and in the glow he saw Loni clutching Pete
around his waist. Pete's face was black from
playing in the cave; Loni's was white.

Mike turned and shone the light in the other
direction. Ten feet ahead the tunnel sloped up
and widened. Scrambling on all fours, he
crossed the distance in seconds.

He knelt at the wider opening and flashed
the light again. A backpack and the remains of
a picnic lay in the beam. Two dozen toy Indians stood ready for battle; comic books were

scattered in the sand. Mike moved the light and saw his brother.

Buddy was slumped against the cave wall. He looked like a stuffed doll that someone had forgotten to put away.

Mike crawled into the cave. His knee landed on something hard. He reached to remove the rock, but it wasn't a rock. It was an insulin bottle, partly empty.

Mike shook Buddy's shoulder, gently. His skin felt warm through the T-shirt.

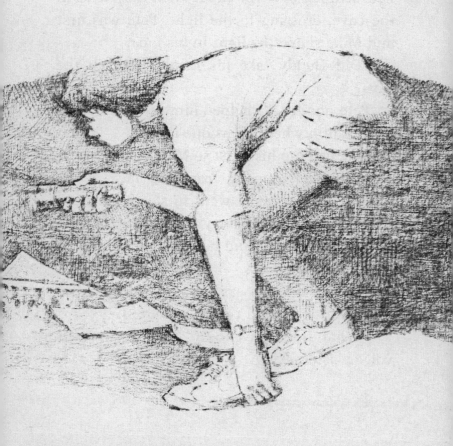

"Buddy, wake up. Buddy, it's me, Mike—come on, wake up!"

Buddy's head rolled toward Mike. His mouth opened slightly, but his eyes stayed shut.

Mike turned and yelled back into the tunnel. "Loni quick, I need you!" He heard her and Pete scuffing over the sand. Then they were in the cave, crossing to the light. Pete was first and Mike shone the light in his face.

"Did Buddy take his insulin shot in the cave?"

Pete nodded. "I helped him do it. He made me tell him when it was one-thirty."

Pete held up his wrist so Mike could see the red numbers glowing from the face of his watch. "Then he just went to sleep and I got scared." Pete started to cry again. "He stuck the needle into his leg and he was talking and he went to sleep."

Mike held Pete's arm up and looked closer at his watch. It said two-thirty-seven.

"What did he have to eat?" Mike asked. His voice was cracking.

"A banana, some potato chips, and peanut butter and crackers."

"Any soda?"

"No," Pete said. "We brought Cokes, but Buddy never drank his. He was in a hurry to get his shot."

Mike spun around and found the pack; one Coke can was unopened. He yanked the top off and crawled back to Buddy. Thrusting the flashlight into Pete's lap, he slipped one hand behind Buddy's neck. His head felt heavy.

"Open his mouth," Mike said to Loni. She did, and he poured the warm foamy liquid between Buddy's lips. Buddy choked and spit up the Coke. Mike repeated the pouring until he was sure his brother was swallowing more than he was spilling over his chin.

Mike stared at his brother's dirty face. Even with Loni and Pete kneeling next to him, he felt very alone.

9

The next five minutes in the dank, close cave seemed like an hour to Mike. The hand supporting Buddy's head was numb, and his neck ached from holding it and his whole body in one position.

Loni knelt next to Mike with her fingers pressed under Buddy's ears where his jaw and neck bones came together. Buddy's mouth hung open as Mike poured small amounts of Coke down his throat. Pete sat Indian style with the beam of the flashlight on Buddy's face.

Nobody spoke because there was nothing to say. Behind them, outside the tunnel, the ocean moaned as it closed in on Bald Head Cliff.

Then, as if he'd been napping and now it was time to get up, Buddy opened his eyes. He blinked and squinted at the light, then slowly recognized the faces above him.

"What's going on?" he asked.

Mike blinked back the tears that were trying to roll down his face. He felt as if he had been sucked into a whirlpool, but now he was floating on a calm lake; the whirlpool had vanished. It took a few seconds for him to realize that the nightmare was finally over.

"You had a reaction," he told Buddy. "How do you feel?"

"A little sleepy." Buddy sat up with Mike's help and looked around. "We're in the cave?"

Mike sat back on his heels; it felt good to move again. "Yes, but we aren't going to stay here talking about it." He took the light from Pete and trained it on Buddy again. "You sure you're okay? We have to get out of here right now."

"I'm okay, honest."

"Let me know if you start to feel funny or

anything." Mike turned and used the light to find the Indians and soldiers. When he began stuffing them into the pack, he found a plastic bag half filled with cookies. He tossed the bag into Buddy's lap. "Eat a few of these," he ordered.

At school Buddy started to fall asleep once and the teacher poured grape juice down his throat. He was fine after the sugar got into his blood. Now, in the cave, Mike hoped for the same miracle.

Loni led them out. Pete came next, then Buddy. Mike followed Buddy so he could keep an eye on him.

They moved quickly. Being smaller, Buddy and Pete were able to scoot along on hands and knees. Mike had a harder time because of the flashlight he held in one hand. As he crawled, the light beam bounced from cave floor to ceiling to walls like a yellow bat.

After a few minutes Buddy stopped; Mike was forced to do the same. "What's the matter?" he called ahead to Loni.

"Water," she yelled back. "I don't know

how deep it is. What should we do?"

Mike thought fast. They couldn't go back, that much was certain. They'd been in the cave about twenty minutes already. Mike knew the tide was slowly covering the mouth of the cave.

"The tunnel slopes down there," he yelled. "We'll have to swim out the last few feet."

"I can swim," Pete said.

"Me too," said Buddy.

Mike shone the light past Buddy until he saw Pete's face peering back at him like a raccoon's.

"Hold onto your sister's feet," Mike told him. "Crawl when she crawls, do everything she does, okay? And don't stop no matter what!"

Pete nodded, the excitement glowing in his eyes.

Mike put his hand on Buddy's back. "Listen, when we get to the end the water will be over our faces. That's because we'll be on our stomachs. Outside it'll only be up to your waist, so don't be afraid, all right?"

He could feel Buddy trembling with excitement and fear. He wondered if the little guy knew *he* was scared, too.

"When the water covers your head, hold your breath and start swimming underwater. I'll be right behind you and I'll push you along."

Mike looked into Buddy's trusting face. Right now he'd drink the ocean if I asked him to, Mike thought, sincerely hoping that wouldn't be necessary.

"We're only going to be underwater for a few feet," Mike added. "Okay?"

"I'm not scared," Buddy said. is voice sounded plenty scared to Mike. At Buddy's age he would have been terrified.

Mike shouted ahead to Loni: "Let's go." He prayed that he was right about how high the water had risen. But it as too late to do anything about that. They had to move on.

Mike stiffened as the cold water swirled around his chest and stomach. He put his hand out to touch Buddy. He knew his brother must be pretty panicky right now, no matter how brave he was acting.

"Don't stop!" Mike yelled ahead, but mostly for his brother. "I'm right behind you; keep going till you're outside."

The rest happened quickly. Mike was shoulder deep in water for an instant. The flashlight, still clutched in his hand, had gone out. One of Buddy's kicking feet smashed into his nose. Mike cried out and choked on a mouthful of salt water. He coughed it out, took a deep breath, and plunged. Now he was totally underwater.

It was black and cold down there. Mike opened his eyes and the salt bit into them; he saw only darkness and darker shadows. He released the dead flashlight and clawed his way forward. His back scraped the tunnel ceiling; he was floating.

Then the gray murk grew lighter. He knew he was seeing sunlight through the water. Kicking and scratching like a trapped animal, Mike shot the last few feet out of the tunnel.

His head smashed into someone's legs. Hands were all over him, yanking him to his knees, then his feet. He lost his balance, fell, was helped up again. The salt stung his eyes shut, but he knew he was outside and safe.

He spit out salt water and wiped his eyes. When he opened them Loni and Pete and Buddy were there with him. The water was at his waist, higher on the others. All around them it swirled, the waves smacking them, forcing them to hold on to each other.

"Come on," Mike cried. He grabbed Buddy under one arm and hurried him toward the cliff. Like seals, they left the water and climbed onto the rocks.

At the top, Buddy huddled against the tree trunk near his bike. Mike lay a few feet away with an arm over his eyes. Pete and Loni sat nearby, leaning against each other's backs.

No one spoke. The desperate swim out of the tunnel and the quick climb up the cliff path had left them drained. They shivered until the sun began to dry their hair and clothes.

"Mike? What made me fall asleep in the cave?" Buddy asked. He had lost one sneaker and was yanking a tube sock higher on his ankle.

Mike raised his head slowly. In only a few minutes the sun had begun to put him to sleep. He blinked and glanced around at the others. Another time he would have laughed. They all looked as if they'd just swum the English Channel.

"I think you needed sugar," Mike said, swinging his eyes to Buddy. "Either that or you got too much insulin in the needle back in the cave."

Mike sat up suddenly. "Where did you get the insulin, anyway?"

Buddy looked embarrassed. "I took it from the upstairs bathroom. When you didn't come home, Pete and me decided to come to the cave to play. He has a watch so I knew I could take my shot on time." He looked from his brother to Loni. "Didn't you see my note?"

"What note ."

"I wrote down where we were going and stuck it on the refrigerator," Buddy said.

Mike shook his head. "I was in the kitchen three times but I didn't see any note." He remembered how crazy he'd acted when he first found Buddy missing.

"It was still pretty stupid," Mike blurted, trying to keep his voice from showing how angry and scared he was. "You were told to wait, Buddy."

Buddy stared at his lone sneaker. "We left a note," he repeated, beginning to cry.

"I was looking for *you*, not a dumb *note*," Mike said, raising his voice. Pete looked as if he was going to start crying too.

"Let's go," Mike muttered.

Loni and Pete rode ahead. When he and Buddy were alone, Mike stopped his bike. "I'm sorry I wasn't home when you got there," he said. "The game took longer than I thought. I'm really sorry."

"That's okay." Buddy spun one pedal with the toe of his sneaker. When it stopped spinning he looked at Mike. "You going to tell Mom and Dad?"

"They already know," Mike answered. "Mom called home about an hour ago and I told her you were missing."

Buddy spun the pedal again.

"We've just got to face it," Mike said. "We messed up and they're going to be plenty mad and there's nothing we can do about it."

He watched Buddy's face working and tried to imagine what was going on inside his little brother's brain. "Look, don't worry about that now, okay? Let's just get home."

Buddy's face changed again. This time it grew solemn. He found his balance and pedaled furiously along the sandy path toward home. His bottom, high in the air, was still wet.

Mike yawned. He knew the day wasn't over yet by a long shot. His parents weren't going to be easy on him—or his brother. He pressed a tired foot onto its pedal and followed Buddy.

Overhead, a lone sea gull hovered, staring down at the procession of bikes. Mike wondered if it was Seabreeze.

10

M*ike* and Buddy were waiting together on the porch when their parents pulled up in the station wagon.

After a confusing mixture of hugs and angry questions, they all went into the kitchen. Mike poured everyone a tall glass of lemonade. Mr. and Mrs. Sanders sat twirling ice cubes in their glasses and listened as first Mike and then Buddy told what had happened while they were away.

Mike never took his eyes off Buddy, sitting across from him at the table. Buddy's lips quivered a few times, especially when he got to the part about the decision to go to the cave. But he never pulled his nobody-loves-me act.

When Buddy finished talking, the kitchen became quiet. Mike peered at his parents from under his eyebrows, and for once he couldn't read their faces. His mother's was white from anger or fear—probably both. His father's face showed nothing, unless you counted the blinking of his eyes.

Buddy broke the silence. "Are you going to punish us?"

"Do *you* think you should be punished?" his mother asked.

"I think we both deserve it," Mike said, taking Buddy off the hook. "But especially me. I was wrong to leave Buddy at Pete's house and I was wrong for getting home late." His fingers were shaking as he drew lines in the condensation on the side of his glass. "I'm sorry, Buddy," he said.

Buddy sat up straight in his chair. He looked his father in the eye. "Whatever you do to Mike, you have to do it to me, too. Pete and me should have stayed here and waited, no matter how late Mike was."

He sneaked a glance at Mike before going on. "We were glad you didn't come on time because we knew if you did we couldn't go to the cave." Now he looked directly at Mike. "I'm sorry, too."

No one spoke for a long moment. Mike had a lump in his throat the size of a baseball.

"As far as blame is concerned," Mike's father said, reaching out to touch Buddy's hand, "your mother and I were wrong in agreeing to leave you, knowing that Mike had a busy morning planned." He glanced at his wife. "For that *we* apologize to both of *you*."

"What about our punishment?" Buddy asked again.

His parents exchanged looks, but this time they were smiling. "I can't imagine any punishment greater than what you two have been through already today," Mike's father said. His voice had gotten husky. "We're just so thankful you're both safe."

"But," added Mike's mother as she reached for the empty glasses, "if you insist on being punished, how about spending an hour cleaning your rooms? The board of health wants to condemn the whole top floor."

Buddy scampered up the stairs as if he'd been shot from a cannon. His mother went outside with her husband to carry in the day's treasures.

Mike sat at the table and thought about calling Loni Anderson. They'd shared so much that day—he felt like talking it over.

Maybe she won't want to talk to me, Mike realized as he went to the phone. Maybe she'll hang up. After all, I did get her into a whole lot of trouble.

He dialed anyway. "Hi, Loni," he said. "It's Mike."

She didn't hang up.

Mike stretched out on the sofa with the phone on his stomach. "How's your hand?" he asked, grinning into the receiver.

About the Author

Ron Roy lives in Hartford, Connecticut in a Victorian house near Mark Twain's house. He travels every summer and enjoys many outdoor sports, including snorkeling, skin diving, and white water rafting.

Formerly a school teacher, Mr. Roy has written several books for children.

Look for these and other **Apple Paperbacks**
in your local bookstore!

SNOW TREASURE
Mary McSwigan

A story of courage and adventure.

Peter Lundstrom never thought he would become a hero.
But that bleak winter of 1940 was like no other. Nazi troops
parachuted into Peter's tiny village and held it captive.
Nobody thought they could be defeated — until Uncle
Victor told Peter how the children of the village could fool
the enemy.

It was a dangerous plan. Peter and his friends had to
slip past Nazi guards with nine million dollars in gold hidden
on their sleds. It meant risking their country's treasure —
and their lives.

ISBN 0-590-33992-3 $2.25US/$2.95CAN

THE MYSTERY AT PEACOCK PLACE

M.F. Craig

No one ever goes near the old Peacock mansion. . . .

Hobie and his dog Shadow didn't mean to trespass on old Miss Peacock's property. But when Shadow tears off after a rabbit, Hobie just has to go after him — even if it means getting into trouble.

What Hobie sees through the window of the Peacock mansion is enough to scare anyone. Hobie's sure something strange is going on, but his best friend Ben is too busy taking care of his horse to help him unravel the mystery.

So Hobie's got to do it alone, though Sheriff Higher warns him not to. But if Hobie had known what was in store for him that terrible night . . . he might never have gone back to Peacock Place at all!

ISBN 0-590-33295-3 $2.25US/$2.95CAN